Broken

A Novella

Self-published using lulu.com

ISBN# 978-1-105-11072-6

Broken

A Novella

By Lisa Gore

Dedication

I want to dedicate this to my deceased mother who I never had the opportunity to meet. Her story can be found in these pages. My late Grandmother who raised me the best she knew how. Her story can also be found in these pages. And finally to my spiritual mother Sherry Biggs who helped me to truly love my savior and know Him as God. You too are found in these pages. To my readers, may you discover your one true love, God the father through Jesus Christ.

Note from the Author

If ever a book could be fiction and non-fiction at the same time this would be it. Even though not everything in this story took place as written, "What a butterfly" contains many truths and all of the poetry pieces are written from feelings I have expressed throughout my life.

Chapter 1

You use to say you loved me.

Then, when I started to believe,

I realized they were mere words used to deceive.

You use to embrace me and drift away in my eyes.

You use to say such beautiful things,

didn't know they were all lies.

Deception, deceit, confusion, and pain.

You walk with your head held high

as I struggle and strain.

Drowning so deep in my tears,

can't you hear me calling your name?

How does it make you feel, knowing I

cry every night?

How does it make you feel, knowing I will never be right?
How could you destroy me when I've only been true? How
could you make so many promises and never come
through? How can you hold so much hate, when all I did
was love you?

It was a very cold night in Harlem, one of the coldest that season. The trees were naked and the ground cracked from the pressure of the wind. The only cure for the season's pain was summer, but she was long gone.

The door flew open to Unique's home one night at a very untimely hour. As she heard the door lock and the sounds of heavy footsteps travel up the stairs, tears rolled down her raw cheek onto the pillow. Unique had nothing left in her to argue. She had been up all night crying and screaming as she vented. She had the pleasure of a friendly listening ear from her best friend Precious.

"I can't live in this pain anymore!" She cried as Precious listened to her reoccurring story. Emmanuel crept into bed and assumed Unique was fast asleep. He dared to put his arm around her in fear she would wake. He went off to sleep as Unique laid there, still and lifeless. Softly, she cried herself to sleep.

The sun pushed its way through the curtain and morning appeared. Unique wakened with the birds outside her window. She failed to get any real sleep, painful memories crowded her mind. Standing in her full-length mirror, she stared deeply into her eyes as if trying to find herself. It was as if she could actually see the pain in her heart.

"How much, how long?" she whispered as she studied the rest of her body. Emmanuel woke at the sound of her voice. His eyes laid upon her beautiful body as the sun beamed luminous rays onto her girly figure. The bruises on her back and arms were as bright as the morning sun. He turned over and fell back asleep to avoid any discussions. He had run out of answers.

Unique made her way over to the calendar and pondered the days. It appeared strange until she noticed that she had not changed the month. She quietly ripped off January and brought herself up to date. Her fresh and new beginning was supposed to start last month, the beginning of the New Year. Yet, tender words and questionable tears delayed it again. As she got dressed and headed to her office, she said to herself, "today is going to be a good day, no matter what!" Then she hopped into her Lavender Expedition and made her way down the city streets.

I know I said "I forgive you" and I truly believe I do.

However, every now and then, I relive

the smacks you threw. My sweetheart, my

love, are you some man I never knew?

Never thought you would allow your hands to harm

me and inflict such pain, the inner

torn more than the outer and now my heart

appears stained. You have done

very little, roses just weren't enough.

Maybe you should still be saying "I'm sorry"

and trying to make this up. It was easy to

forgive you when sorrow was trapped

in your eyes. But now it's as if it never

happened and we've just moved on with our

lives. Well I discovered today that my heart

still cries. I've tried to see you in the

same light, sometimes it follows through.

Then other times I stare into your eyes

without the faintest clue. You are my lover, my man,

someone I never knew.

Unique entered her office and smiled at everyone with newness in her heart. "Good morning Mark"

"Good morning Ms. James. We just got an order in for five hundred flyers and we are almost out of multicolor paper!"

"It's fine Mark, the shipment is probably just running a little late. You can go to the supply store and get what we need. Let me get settled in and I'll write you a petty cash check."

"Okay" Mark replied.

Unique entered her private office and gazed out of the window at the streets of Manhattan.

"It's going to be a good day no matter what," she repeated in her mind as if she wanted the statement to be embedded in her soul. She wrote out the check for her employee. Buzz!

"Yes Ms. James."

"The check is ready Mark. You can come get it and go to the supply store now."

"I'll be right in Ms. James"

It was about 10:30 am when Unique received a call from Emmanuel.

"Hey pretty how's your day coming along?" She sighed as she took their picture from her desk and

tossed it into the trash.

"Fine, but I'm very busy so let me call you later." Click! She smiled at her great achievement and a heavy weight was lifted from her. She didn't want to give him any room to change what was in her heart. She popped out of her seat as if shackles were being released from her ankles. Buzz! "Yes?"

"Precious come into my office quickly!" The door flew open almost instantly. Precious worked as Unique's assistant and her desk was right outside of her office.

Let me be honest, let me be true.

Let me tell you how my skies are gray, yet they use to shine blue, until there was you. You think you've brought me sunshine, carrying a bag full of sorrow? I ask for sunshine and you say, "There's tomorrow" Well tomorrow never came, even though it was yesterday. Now I am use to the darkness, the rain and pain, love to give, no love to gain. However, you think you're my butter to my bread, my sheets to my bed, yet my heart will continue to beat, even if it is not red. Did you hear what I said? You don't complete me, no man does! Did you think this was some great love that never was? Is this all that I'm worth, the best that I can do? I settle for pennies instead of hundreds, gray skies instead of blue.

Something is blocking my sunshine,

that something is you!

"What crazy lady! What is it?"

"I have some serious cleaning out to do today so I'm going to leave early. If you need me call me, okay?"

"Okay girl", Precious swung her hips from right to left.

"I'll hold it down here and you go do what you have to do!"

"You're the best Precious, and I'm sorry for keeping you up all night."

"Anytime girl" Precious always prayed that Unique would build up enough courage and self-esteem to leave Emmanuel. Now the day was here.

"Praise God!" she shouted.

Unique went down to the basement of her building and gathered some big construction trash bags and boxes. She loaded them into the back of her SUV then headed home. Music blasting, Unique sang her heart out, "I'm not gon cry, I'm not gon cry, I'm not gon shed no tears." She smiled as people stared into her vehicle and tried to figure out who she was talking to. Her heart had lightness to it for the first time in years. Finally, she felt that her smile would shine again and life was not meant to always be painful. She sat at the red light and waited patiently for it to change. Errrrr... BAM! Out of nowhere, a red pick-up truck plunged straight into her side of her SUV. The airbag popped out, yet the impact was so great that she blacked out instantly. She was not wearing her seatbelt. She would have had it on but she was rushing home and didn't take the time to buckle up. When the paramedics arrived, they rushed her to the nearest hospital.

She was rolled into the E.R. and worked on right away. The Doctor who cared for Unique could not believe his eyes. He struggled to catch his breath at the sight of her.

"Unique James" he thought to himself. He had not laid eyes on her since high school. Unique was one of the popular ones, but not by choice. Yet, even still, she never noticed someone like David Sharp, the nerd who was always in class on time. He was the unpopular church boy who didn't get into any trouble. She never knew he existed.

Unique was stabilized and if it had not been for the airbag, she could have been seriously hurt. The nurses tried to notify someone from home, but there was no answer. Doctor Sharp kept her overnight for observations and hoped someone would come to pick her up the following day.

The next morning when Unique came to, she wasn't aware of anything; she jumped up and looked around quickly with fear and confusion. She couldn't figure out why she had been brought to a hospital.

"What happened?" She screamed. The nurse made her way to Unique's bedside.

"Well good morning, Ms. James, I'm glad to see that you've come around. You were in a horrible accident with a drunk driver. He's in police custody. Praise God you're Ok! Let me get your Doctor and inform him that you're awake."

Unique sat silently in a state of shock and dropped her head back to the pillow.

"One minute I was on my way home to start packing Emmanuel's things, now here I am in a hospital bed totally lost." She grabbed the sheets to fully cover herself as Dr. Sharp entered the room. He appeared to be very disturbed. "Hello Unique, I'm Dr. Sharp."

"Hello." She responded very quietly. He took a seat next to the bed. "I'm sorry to come to you with this disturbing news but…" he paused. "We were only able to save one of your babies. I am so sorry."

Unable to move or respond, Unique sat quietly in disbelief. "Babies?" She said to herself softly under her breath. At that moment, Dr. Sharp received a page over the intercom for an emergency. He jumped out of the chair quickly.

"Unique I think you will be fine. None of your injuries were serious, yet because you did miscarry one of the babies, I want you to stay another night for observation. Then you'll come back in a week for a follow up. I'll see you a little later." Dr. Sharp rushed out.

"Thank you Doctor!" Unique's feet fell to the floor as if they were a ton of bricks. She felt as though her shackles had just been reattached to her ankles. She took a few steps to the mirror, slowly she studied herself closely. This body of hers that she didn't even know. She longed to get rid of Emmanuel, now it seemed that he would be a part of her forever. For years she tried to get pregnant by him and failed. She assumed she couldn't have children. Now here she was, wanting to leave, yet, bound to stay. She cried and cried. Too depressed to call anyone, she looked out of the window until the sun fell from the sky.

The following morning Unique called Precious to come and pick her up. Nurse Leairah came in and helped Unique get herself together. She gave her all of her information and paper work then wheeled her down to the waiting area.

"You do have someone to pick you up?"

"Yes, thank you so much", Unique smiled.

Nurse Leairah pulled a chair up beside her.

"I'll just wait with you until they arrive." Nurse Leairah knew that Dr. Sharp was very fond of Unique and that bothered her deeply. She was in love with Dr. Sharp, yet even in all her beauty, he wouldn't even give her the time of day. She couldn't understand why and every day she went out of her way to grab some of his attention.

Nurse Leairah handed Unique a drink of water, but she didn't drink it. She hoped a man was coming to pick Unique up. That way her chances with Dr. Sharp could still exist. Unique sat in silence while her thoughts crowded and flooded her baffled mind.

"I'm six weeks pregnant, miscarriage- twins. This is crazy!" On and on her mind wondered. Everything seemed to be still around her.

"Twenty-nine years old, I'm too young for this? Why me. Why by him!"

Dr. Sharp stood at the window in the break room on the 3rd floor of the hospital and watched Unique from afar. Her beauty mesmerized him and he always knew she had a huge heart for people. From the moment they rushed her in, until she woke up, he watched over and took such care of her.

"Wow. I know there's no use, she is obviously taken or does not believe," he said to himself as he sighed.

About ten minutes went by and Precious came running into the hospital.

"Girl are you alright? Why didn't anyone call me? I rang your cell all night and I stopped by your house!"

"I don't know Precious, I'm just coming around myself."

Nurse Leairah got up to leave as she frowned inwardly. "Ms. James please take good care of yourself and get plenty of rest. I'll see you next week."

"Thank you, I will. Bye now." Precious helped Unique out of the wheel chair and into the car.

"What on earth happened to you from point A to point B?"

Unique just shook her head.

"Where do I begin girl, where do I begin?"

"How about from the moment you left me! That sounds like a good place to start". Precious screamed with sarcasm.

Nurse Leairah entered Dr. Sharp's office. "Dr. What are we doing for lunch today? Did you want to grab a bite?"

"No I'm skipping lunch today, thank you though," he said as he continued to look over his work, not allowing his eyes to give her short skirt and long legs any attention. If it wasn't for his obvious attraction to Unique, Nurse Leairah would have assumed the Doctor was gay. Why else would he ignore her every advance?

On the ride back to Unique's home, she told

Precious everything that she remembered about the accident. Yet, she left out the pregnancy and miscarriage. She was not sure if she would keep her baby or not and she didn't need Precious pushing her religious beliefs on her. She had experienced enough. For so long she had dreamed of being a mother, but not this way. She wanted a family for her child, not a monster like Emmanuel. Unique found a way to let the conversation flow in another direction.

"Listen child; let me tell you how my Doctor was hot!"

"Oh was he now?" They laughed. "Well, forget what he looked like, was he saved?" They pulled into Unique's driveway and Unique got out of the car.

"Girl please, I don't know all that, but to say he looked good would be an understatement. I mean, he makes you want to get sick!" They laughed, but deep inside Precious feared for Unique's soul. The trunk opened.

"Well I guess you will be needing these bags after all." She showed her the boxes and bags for Emmanuel's things.

"It's time to make room for some improvements." Unique hugged Precious with an embrace that was full of compassion and her tears rushed down her face.

"Thank you Precious. You are the best. You look out for me more than me."

Precious took the boxes and bags up to the porch and waited for Unique to open the door.

"Unique look, after all that you've done for me, it's only right. I will never be able to do enough. You didn't have to help me so much when I was down and..."

"Look, stop. Unique interrupted. "I've done what I've done because you are my best friend. That is a priceless gift within itself. Besides, I may have the gift of art, but organization is far from me. I needed you to come and make things run right. What would Unlimited Arts be without you?"

"Whatever girl." smiled Precious.

They went into the house and started to pack

Emmanuel's things. Unique knew that he had not been

home because there weren't any dirty dishes in the sink or

dirty clothes on the floor. After they had packed majority of

his belongings, she checked her answering machine. There

were three messages, all from Emmanuel. Beep!

"Hey baby it's your man. I guess you spent the night with

your girl so I won't bother yall. Just get with me." Beep!

"Hey pretty. I was just calling back to see if you had come

in, but I guess its girls night out." CLICK! Unique laughed

and laughed.

   "Yea, now I don't come home and there's a little

problem right!" Precious just shook her head as she silently

prayed while her eyes opened.

   Unique lined all of his bags by the door and then sat

down because she began to have pain.

"I'll do the rest girl, you chill. It's not as if his broke behind has a lot of stuff anyway. Most of this is really yours that you gave to his tired butt!" Beep! The third message played

"A... Unique, Nique, pick up this phone! Pick up the phone! I know you're not at work or with Precious because I called your office. What's going on? You out there acting like a little nasty slut? I'm on my way home right now!" The tone in his voice removed the smile from her face and she sat still and frozen. It was as if he was standing right there screaming down her neck. Emmanuel always had problems with trusting women because his mother was a drug addict. She treated Emmanuel with hate because his father left her when she was pregnant with him. It didn't help matters when Emmanuel grew up to look just like him. As he grew up, he watched countless men rape, use, and abuse his mother. She poured all of her attention into her boyfriends and neglected him and his sisters. It was extremely hard for him to trust Unique because she was so beautiful, she could have any man she wanted. He knew that she could do better than him, and his worst fear was that one day she would believe it.

Precious saw the fear over take Unique and tried to comfort her. "Listen, it's good that he is on his way. We're almost done packing and he can just take his trash and keep getting up. If you want I'll sit his stuff out on the porch and you don't even have to see him." Just then, Emmanuel kicked in the front door.

Chapter 2

As he entered, he couldn't help but notice all of the bags and boxes lined up beside the door.

"So what's this? You were gonna just leave and not say nothing? You dumb little whore! You think he can love you better than me?"

Unique stood to her feet appearing to be brave because she had Precious there with her.

"Leave? Where am I going, this is my house. You are the one that is leaving."

"I'm not going nowhere," Emmanuel screamed. "What, you done found some punk that said he's gonna love you? Hanh? Hanh?" Emmanuel started toward Unique and Precious jumped in between them. "Look Precious, I know she's your girl and all, but this ain't got nothing to do with you." Precious stood in front of Unique, "This is my friend and if..." Unique interrupted her.

"Precious I got this, trust me."

"Yea, I trusted you to handle this last time and you ended up black and blue!" Emmanuel stood over Precious in a bully like manner.

"Look girl you need to get out while you can, unless you want to know what it feels like to have your back stomped out too. Jesus won't be able to save you then!" Emmanuel was filled with rage. Unique pulled Precious out of the house. They came to the porch and Unique gave her a hug.

"I know you love me girl and I know you care, but I have to do this by myself. Just wait in the car for me and I'll be out. I'm going to say what I have to say, then, I'm going to leave and give him the rest of the day to get out. If he is still here later on tonight, I'll call the police and have him removed."

"Okay Nique, but if he starts something,"

"I know Precious. I know."

Regardless of what Unique said, Precious knew better. She got right on her cell phone and called the police. When Unique went back into her house, Emmanuel had punched holes in the walls and was screaming.

"It ain't over you stupid whore! It ain't over!"

"Emmanuel please! Please just go, I can't take this anymore! I can't live with you cheating and beating on me. Time after time you say you'll never hit me, but then what happens?" Emmanuel dropped to his knees beside her feet and broke out into tears.

"I won't, I won't ever put my hands on you again. I can't live without you Unique."

"But that's not all. You go out with other females, you don't want to work, and you don't want to clean. You constantly accuse me of cheating on you when I never have! You were not like this in the beginning. You sold me a lie Emmanuel; I thought I was getting the truth. You have to go and I need to move on. You don't want to change and I can't make you. No more bruises, no more diseases, no more lies, I'm done! Get your things and go. Please don't make this harder than it already is, please."

As Unique headed for the doorway, grief tried to swallow her heart. Emmanuel whaled and cried on the floor in his puddle of tears. She wanted to run back and hold him. She wanted to believe that her promise of closure had made him change. But this time she had to believe that his tears were just a trick to keep her. Something within her said, "Keep walking you are almost free".

Then the phone rang. She didn't move to answer it and he watched her in confusion. The answering service came on and it was Doctor Sharp calling to remind her of her appointment. He sounded concerned and interested, a little too friendly in Emmanuel's eyes. As Unique went for the doorknob, he grabbed her by her ponytail and slung her to the floor. "You think you just gonna walk out! I said I can't live without you!" Unique screamed and cried with everything she had left in her.

"Stop! No!" She tried with all her might to crawl to her freedom, yet she believed she had given it up by staying so long and it would not be back to rescue her. Safety was on the other side of her door, yet it seemed miles away. Emmanuel blocked out her cries completely. He continued to kick and beat on her with stomps and punches full of rage.

"Stop Emmanuel, you're going to kill the baby! Please just let me go!" He did not give her words any power; he acted as if she couldn't speak. Tears and blood were everywhere. He kicked her in her back, stomped on her with his boots and held her down to endure it.

Finally, she managed to kick him between his legs and he dropped to the floor. She crawled to the doorway and saw the Police pull up. They made a call for an ambulance to transport Unique to the hospital. She had been beaten so badly. As Unique was being put into the ambulance, Precious screamed and cried out toward Emmanuel as he sat in the back seat of the cops car.

"You Devil! Only God can help you!" The police took Emmanuel off to jail.

As they approached the hospital, Unique realized it was the same hospital that she was recently released from. There was an officer right there when they took her out of the ambulance. She got off of the cot before they could wheel her in. "I'm okay from here."

"But Miss, we need you to fill out a report."

"I didn't call you guys, and I don't want to file a report. I don't want to press charges; I just want this to be over!" Precious had a look of disbelief on her face as she stood in silence.

"Well at least let me help you into the emergency room."

"I have my friend; I'll be fine, thank you for everything." They walked into the E.R.

"Precious, I need to use the bathroom. Just sign me in; I'll be back in a second." Precious was so mad at her that she could hardly get her words together. "But..."

"I'm fine Precious really." Hunched over, she walked into the bathroom and cleaned herself up. She was too embarrassed to return to the same hospital and risk Dr. Sharp seeing her beaten up by her deranged old boyfriend.

"If I show up like this he won't even consider me," she said to herself as she wiped her face off. She left out of the hospital and took a cab to St. Matthews Hospital not too far from where she was. She was treated and released. There was no harm done to her baby, but the Doctor that treated her advised her to get a restraining order to protect herself and her unborn child. It was clear to even a blind man that she was a battered woman.

Unique took a cab to her office to be alone. Everyone had gone home for the day. She believed that was the safest place for her to be. They wouldn't hold Emmanuel long without her pressing any charges. Unique called Precious on her cell phone. "Hello!"

"Precious I'm sorry."

"What are you doing Unique? How did you get there! I'm sitting here thinking they called you to be seen!"

"Just come here with me. I'm not coming back to the hospital, I'm okay. I went to St. Matthews down the street."

"Girl please! You were bleeding and…"

"I'm not anymore, Trust me I'm okay! Just get here when you can." CLICK!

Precious flew to the office immediately. Unique explained why she left the hospital, but Precious was really irked. "Look sis, I love and care for you very much, but I can't continue to try to help you unless you are going to be honest with me. I'm leaving my family to come assist you, the least you can do is be honest with me." Unique agreed. She asked for her forgiveness and they left. She stayed the night with Precious.

Unique watched Precious as she got dinner together for her family. Tears filled her eyes and she longed to have what Precious had. There was love and peace all through the air. No fighting or fussing, it was beautiful. "I guess all the good men are gone," she mumbled under her breath as she left and went to rest without dinner. Her tears soaked the pillow for most of the night until she finally went to sleep.

Unique wanted to tell Precious about the baby, but more and more she had thoughts of having an abortion and she knew Precious would be totally against that. Precious insisted that Unique take some time off to herself and reassured her that she'd handle everything for a couple of weeks back at the office.

"I will work with Stacy on the gift baskets and Mark will be fine with the orders for the invitations and stuff. You just relax and get your thoughts straight. Here is your planner and I will get the truck out of the shop for you this weekend. Now I gotta go, you know me and Mondays do not get along."

As Precious left Unique smiled and screamed out the door, "Thank you best friend in the world!"

Precious usually only worked part time so she'd have savings and extra spending money. She'd also work for Unique when she needed to take a vacation or time off.

The next morning Unique returned to her house. Everything was still a mess. She had the desire to clean but not the strength. She wondered if her pregnancy would have changed Emmanuel to be a better person. She fell asleep for the rest of that day and dreamed all night long. She dreamed that she had the perfect family like Precious. In her dream, her husband was Dr. David Sharp and they had two beautiful twin boys. They were happy and deeply in love. The dream seemed so real, as if it were a vision.

Morning came and Unique had to get ready for her doctor's appointment. She was so excited about seeing Dr. Sharp again. Her dream had given her hope. She turned on her music and made her way to the closet to study her wardrobe. She spent about ten minutes there and tried to figure out what she would wear to catch his eye.

"Ah yes, my all black dress has never failed me yet!" She slid into her black elegant spandex dress with sheer sleeves, following that were some very sexy knee high pointed toe boots. When she arrived at the hospital, she made it a point to let Dr. Sharp see her before she had to get into that ugly hospital gown.

"Hello Dr. I know I'm a little early but…"

"Oh no it's fine Ms. James. You can go in this room right here and I'll be with you in a moment."

"Okay" she smiled. While she waited for her check-up, she sat with her hospital gown held as tight as she could grasp it. Dr. Sharp and Nurse Leairah made their way into the room. "Hello again Ms. James.

"Dr. Please call me Unique."

"Okay Unique, but only if you will call me David." They both smiled. Nurse Leairah almost cried she was so jealous. While he examined her body, he noticed new bruises. He had seen her bruised arms and back when she came to the hospital the first time and knew that she was being abused.

Saddened by what he found, Dr. Sharp could not understand how a woman who had so much going for her could put up with such madness.

"How could someone who was so strong and smart in high school be so weak now," he wondered silently. After the check-up was over, Dr. Sharp sat down in the chair next to the bed. "So how are you and the baby feeling? Are you having any pain or bleeding?" He placed his hand on her stomach.

"We are fine. No problems at all." There was no way she was going to tell him about her last beating. Little did she know, he already knew.

I'm sorry. I love you. This won't happen again. The lies keep coming and the beatings never end. They say it's the last time; you have to know it's not true. He just wants you to stay, and that's just what you do. Why must we be so weak, it should never reach this length? Why can't we be a little strong, just enough to find strength? You don't like to be abused, the beatings you hate. You keep saying one day you'll leave, but one day may be too late. You won't just be leaving him, but this whole entire world. All because he couldn't stop beating you girl! Are you afraid to leave and fear what he may do? You feel so dead inside, he's already killing you. Yes, you love this man but you must think of your health. How can you truly love him when you're not loving yourself? You believe you deserve better, yet you continue to stay, hoping and praying that he will change one day. With GOD, all things are possible, a man can change. But if you never let him go, he's bound to be the same. Leaving is hard; I know this is not an easy task. But you will rejoice when you are freed, and the bad days have passed.

Dr. Sharp got out of his chair and went towards the door. "Nurse Leairah could you give us a moment alone please?"

"Sure" she said as she stormed out.

"How long have you lived with this hidden pain?" Unique was so embarrassed she couldn't even open her mouth to speak. "How long has he been beating on you?"

"What do you mean?" She responded with embarrassment.

"Unique, I know the bruises you had when you came in after the car accident were not from the crash. I see this all the time. Is he your husband?"

"No never!" She screamed and brushed away some of her tears and made room for the new ones. "It's over. We are so over. I just thought he would stop. I wanted to believe he would stop, but it only got worse. I can't believe I'm even telling you this, I'm so embarrassed."

"Look" he took her hand and placed it between both of his. "We all do things we regret; no one can say anything about the next person. We all sin and we all make crazy mistakes. As long as you realize it and get out, you're on your way. So are you feeling okay now? How bad did he hurt you?"

"Well I have been in a great deal of pain, but..." Dr. Sharp's facial expression spoke his deep concern. He called in a few nurses and laid Unique down on the bed. They ran her through a great deal of test and realized she was now in danger of losing her other baby. She was not aware of all that was going on because of the medication they had given her.

Finally, after Unique was stabilized Dr. Sharp came back into the room. "You came very close to losing your baby. Nevertheless, you both are fine now. I'm putting you on bed rest and you can't work throughout your pregnancy. You will be released in the morning, but for now just rest."

He could have sent her home then but he was so afraid for her and not knowing what kind of man she was dealing with, he just wanted to protect her as much as possible. Unique didn't respond with words only with her eyes. Deep down inside she felt sad that she didn't lose the baby because it meant forever Emmanuel, forever pain. And as for making an impression on Dr. Sharp, she just knew she had blown that. She fell fast asleep.

Chapter 3

Morning crept its way into her sight and right beside her on the nightstand was a big vase with a dozen of pink and white roses. She picked up the card. "Unique, these Beautiful new roses represent your beautiful new beginning! Stay encouraged and may God Bless your soul. Until we meet again.

Sincerely,

The man you never knew, who always knew you,

Dr. David Sharp (212) 543-0302"

"Always knew me," she thought to herself. "What is he trying to say to me?" She called Precious to come and get her and gave her all the information on her latest events, yet she still didn't mention a word about the baby.

Later that night Unique got a knock at her door. "That's Strange. I know my bell is working", she thought to herself as she made her way to the front door. She looked out and saw it was Emmanuel. He had tears in his eyes and something in his hands. She didn't open the door and stood there in silence. Emmanuel knocked for two more minutes, and then he stuck two envelopes in her mail slot and walked off with his head held down in shame. The smell of the letters caused her to shiver because it had her favorite cologne sprayed on them. She opened the first envelope and it was a card. She read it as she went back up the stairs.

"I'm so sorry. The inside read: *I've really messed up, this is so true. And now my heart cries from the pain I've caused you. Is there anything I can say, anything I can do? Please take our love back and let's start at brand new."*

Tears rolled down her face and faded Emmanuel's name off of the card. She was carrying his child and there was nothing she wanted more than for things to work, but she was too afraid. It was always so hard to leave him. Although he was a beast, he had a great gentle side as well. She felt her heart getting weak for him and she ripped up the card and refused to read what was in the other envelope and ripped that up as well. She cried all night long until her tears were dry.

Morning hit the sky and she was looking forward to a relaxing day. There was a message on her answering machine. BEEP! "Unique I hope you'll forgive me for being unprofessional and calling you, but I wanted to know if you liked the flowers I left you and did you understand my note. If you would like some clarity on it, give me a call. Feel better and I'll see you soon."

There was no doubt in David's mind that Unique was attracted to him. That's why he did not hesitate to give her a call. I mean after all, who comes to see their Doctor in a hot black dress? Unique called Precious and told her about the message.

"What did you say his name was again?"

"David Sharp."

"Oh my gosh! Oh my goodness," Precious couldn't believe what she was hearing.

"What!" Unique interpreted.

"It's David Sharp from high school girl! Remember the nerd that always wore that tight Champion sweat suit all year long?"

"No." Unique sat in total confusion.

"Think girl think! He was like the smartest kid in the

school! Remember in our tenth grade gym class when he ripped his shorts and ran out with those polka dot boxers!" Precious struggles to explain through her laughter.

"That is not him Precious!"

"Girl it is. Go look in your year book and call me back."
They hung up and Unique went to search for her yearbook.
It was him for sure! Unique went out to her porch laughing
hysterically to get her newspaper and there sat Emmanuel.
She jumped back with fear.

"I'm not gonna hurt you Nique, I just want to talk a little.
Did you get my letters?" It was as if his mouth was just
moving and no words were coming out. All she could think
about was how he stomped and beat her. She also blamed
him for the accident because she knew if she had not been
coming home to kick him out, she would not have crossed
paths with that drunk driver. Unique pulled her bath rode
together tightly and stepped back into the house. Rage
filled her whole being. "I'm Pregnant! And when you
stomped my back out you almost killed our second baby! I
was pregnant with twins until I got into that accident!"
Emmanuel stood still in disbelief. "Yea, the night you
thought I was out having fun I was lying up in the hospital.
I screamed at you and told you I was pregnant, but you just
wouldn't stop beating on me long enough to hear what I
was saying!" Tears flooded her face as she struggled to
catch her breath. Emmanuel fell to his knees.

"No! No! I.......I...." His words could not come together and
he started to cry. "I'm so sorry. I didn't know baby! I didn't
know! I won't ever take you through pain like that again.

When I was locked up that night, these guys found out why I was in and they kicked my behind, all three of them. One of the guys stomped me so hard that he broke one of my ribs. I felt what it was like and I couldn't believe I was doing that to you. Nique please let us be a family. I promise I will never lay a hand on you again for as long as I live. Please," he begged through all of his tears.

Can I be loved as I was before? Should I start over again, or would that just hurt more? Can I leave the Past behind and forget how I felt?

Should I fall in love again, or just stay to myself? Could I with stand the pain if he hits me again? Should I hang up my heart and not have a boyfriend? I give my all; in return, I get hurt. I don't gain one thing from all of my hard work. Should I seek advice, or just rely on what I know. Can't stand it here with him, can't bear to let him go.

The power of his anguish was so strong and convincing. Her love for him was still very much alive and her dream seemed as though it could have been coming true. She began to feel so sorry for Emmanuel. After all, his mother and father never showed him how to love. She believed he was trying to love; he just needed her to teach him. She started to cry along with him and fell to the floor.

"But I'm going to have an abortion, I can't handle this. I don't trust you Manny, I can't". Emmanuel refused to stop begging and he cried a river of tears. His heart was sincere but what was truth? He'd been scarred and was not aware of his need for true help. Nevertheless, after ten minutes of pleading, Unique would once again open a door that was supposed to stay shut. "Okay Emmanuel, please stop crying. I still love you and I want you... just don't hurt me again, I can't take it if..."

"I won't Unique, I promise you. My promise is real this time baby. I don't want to lose you again." With fear and doubt, she took him back once again. Unique's love for Emmanuel blotted out her common sense and she decided to try one more time for her unborn child's sake. Her decision was based on what her heart felt and not what her mind knew to be a fact. She blocked David's phone number so he could never call again and accepted that this would be her life.

Can you be deeply in love, yet hate it so much?

Can you long to be held, yet hate to be touched?

Can you be in love, yet confused by your feelings?

Can you want to start again, but not truly be willing?

*Can you cry and cry, endure and endure, then let the same
one that hurt you, come back to hurt you even more?*

Can you pretend to be fine, yet be dying inside?

*Can your life be so happy, then in a moment you wished
that you died?*

Can you love the same or will it be different?

Can your love be returned if you already sent it?

*Can you be so hurt and confused that you can't even see
this so-called place "In Love" is not where you should be?*

Chapter 4

A few months went by and everything appeared to be fine. They had a few arguments here and there, but nothing major. Unique was busy planning things for their new baby and Emmanuel stayed out mostly. He promised he'd find a job before the baby arrived. Unique was going on her fifth month of pregnancy, yet she still was not showing.

Precious was disappointed and so hurt that Unique never told her about the babies. Yet and still, she was there for Unique because she loved her. She just accepted what was, but she never understood how Unique could settle for less.

Precious went to church on a weekly basis and always prayed about Unique and her situation, but Unique had no interest in church or God at all. No one taught her about God when she was growing up. Her mother died when she was only two years old. Her father tried to be a dad to her but somehow his drug addiction and lust for women kept getting in the way. Therefore, after being abused mentally and physically for years by him, at the age of fourteen she found a job and began to raise herself. She moved out at 16 and rented a room from an older lady in her neighborhood. Unique continued to attend school and although she was very popular, she was very shy and kept to herself. She feared that if anyone were to find out her situation they would report her and she would end up in foster care or worst.

Somehow Unique made it through those difficult years of high school. She wanted to pray for help, but she didn't know how to begin. No one ever told her about GOD until she meet Precious. They knew each other in the ninth grade, but it wasn't until the tenth grade that they became best friends. Unique knew she could trust her with her housing secret and Precious never told a soul.

Precious told Unique about Jesus and what He had done for mankind. She tried to believe, but the whole concept seemed pointless in her eyes. Precious continued to pray for Unique, hoping and believing GOD would one day change her heart, but she never forced her to do anything.

As I sit and slowly watch you, sadly I see you killing yourself. I crave to extend you my help. But you have to want it and need it. If you have no cry, how can I relieve it? Down goes your head sinking slowly, tangled and tied unable to be freed. Do you want to be saved, then you must first believe. You can float to the surface, but you must feel the need. How long can your soul stop its breath? Will you reach out while there is still time, or wait until there's none left? I can't jump in to help if you plan to remain, in your tangled web that you wove, which is causing such pain.

Just know I am here waiting, praying, with hope and believing, you'll one day accept my helpful heart, for it's never leaving. As the wet drops roll down my cheeks, and hit the water from which you reach, I long to rescue you lost one who is so weak. But it's your call, your case, your option, and your place, your belief, your faith, but you can be saved!

Emmanuel and Unique were getting along and the beatings were a thing of the past. Unique often thought about Dr. Sharp and what might have been but she never called him. But she never threw his note with his phone number away either and it remained in her draw.

One day while Emmanuel was looking for something, he came across the note and was heated with anger. The trust that he never was able to have in the first place was instantly and permanently destroyed at that moment. He became enraged as he punched the wall repeatedly.

"She hates me! Why would she do this! I was changing, I was changing!" He couldn't get his self together so he ran out of the house crying, with fury reigning in his limbs.

Later that night Unique inquired about the wall. "What on earth happened Emmanuel?"

"I bought you a picture and I was trying to hang it, man I jacked the wall and the picture up, I'm sorry. I'll fix it in the morning". The lie fell from his mouth with such ease.

"Well where is the picture?" She asked desperately.

"It's in the trash, it was destroyed."

"Thank you anyway sweetie" she kissed his cheek.

About one week later, Unique woke Emmanuel to go to the store for a few things. It had been a while since the crash, yet she was not ready to drive. As she sat and waited for him to return, she realized that if she was ever going to conquer her fear of driving, she had to start at least trying. So, she pumped herself up and threw some clothes on.

"I should go and meet him at the store and surprise him by driving again." She thought to herself. Emmanuel didn't have his driver's license so he walked to the store. She knew she could catch up with him. Unique hopped in her ride and quickly headed to the store. She pulled up, and just as she did, she saw another woman with Emmanuel stuck to her lips! She sped off. So shocked, Emmanuel started to run after her but of course, she left him. She was so distraught that she couldn't even breathe. Her tears blocked her vision and she barely made it home. She went into the house and fell on her bed. All she could think about was how she had to now raise her baby alone. Abortion looked like a very beautiful escape at one point, but now it was just too late. She hated herself for having taken Emmanuel back. In great pain, she fell to the floor. Emmanuel ran into the room.

"Well, you were cheating on me. Now weren't you? I found your little note from David, you stinking tramp! I knew you were playing me! That baby isn't mine either, is it?"

He tried to help her off the floor as evil justifications rolled out of his hateful mouth. She pulled away from him and screamed.

"Get out! Get out! I never want to see you again!

Get out!"

Some people thought I was stupid because I refused let you go. No one was there when you were loving me, so hey, they don't know! Getting over was hard, you mean so much. They act as if I should hate you, well I'll never do such. The love that is in you is not enough for another try. This is the part where I move on, regardless of your cry. I'm not giving up on love; I'm just giving up on you! I've given you my all, and done all that I can do. You've made up your mind; you have chosen your girl. I sure hope she brings happiness to your imbalanced world. I did my very best; no one can say I didn't try.

Now this time it's forever, now this time it's goodbye.

Emmanuel tried to explain, but he could not be heard over the whales of her cries. "I don't need a whore like you any way, you nasty slut!" He left the room, returned with a bottle of beer, and poured it all over her. In his anger, he went about the house and ripped up her clothes, smashed her furniture, and put holes in the walls. Unique just laid there on the cold wet floor as she cried, and cried. He picked up the cordless phone and was getting ready to throw it at her, and then he heard police sirens. He quickly ran out of the back door. He thought Unique called the police on him but she didn't. There was another attack going on in her neighborhood.

When Emmanuel left, he went and lived with the female that he was caught cheating with and that was it. He was gone. Unique cried all through the night. She refused to call Precious and upset her and her beautiful family. Unique dreamed of being in her shoes. "If only for a day" she thought, but Unique never believed she could have that kind of life. She cried herself to sleep with no hope for anything. In the middle of the night, she woke and said a prayer.

"I guess if Precious knows how to find a good man, have a life filled with joy and peace I should listen to her. She says it's connected to you, so I guess we should have a talk God." She prayed until her words sent her to sleep.

I know there are things in my life you must remove from me.

I know there are bumps in my road that only you see.

I realize now that you are with me for

the mountains I must climb. And I could have been over them if I hadn't wasted time. I have this desire inside, it's killing me dead. Just when I thought I had control, it controlled me instead. I have no strength to get up; yes, I lack the strength to stand. Falling into death, instead of following your plan.

So here I am GOD all filthy, yet I want to be right. I want to live in a way that is pleasing to your sight. I give my whole heart to you, I give you my life.

I don't want any parts of it; please just have your way. I want to be changed, please come into my life today.

"Get up! Come on Unique you are bleeding all over the place!" Unique was in a pool of blood all night and did not realize it. Precious was worried and came over because she didn't answer her phone. She wrapped her bath robe around her and drug her to the car. She was so weak from all of the blood she had lost that she couldn't say a word.

Precious rushed her to the hospital and before she could get her out of the car, Unique passed out. Five hours later Unique finally came to and noticed Dr. Sharp and Precious as they stood beside the bed. She overheard them talking about how she had a miscarriage and lost her baby. She closed her eyes and smiled. She didn't want them to know she had heard them so she pretended to still sleep.

She felt free, relieved, and for once in her life she believed GOD had answered her prayers. It wasn't that she didn't want the blessing of a child, but the pain that she believed the child would have to endure was frightening. She thought of GOD as her last resort, yet, He was her greatest decision. She prayed that God would help her and answer her cry. She cried and prayed for relief from a life that was too much to bear. She dreaded bringing Emmanuel's child into the world for him to abuse.

When she opened her eyes a little while later, they told her everything that happened and she reassured them that she would be okay. She grabbed Precious by the hand and said, "all things work together for the good right?"

Precious was shocked that Unique would even say this. Every time she would try to encourage her with this scripture when she was going through a crisis, she thought Unique never really listened. They cried and held each other. Dr. Sharp quietly left the room and she did not see him for the rest of her stay. Unique was released the following day and went home.

About two months later, Unique went into her draw and pulled out Dr. Sharp's note that had his name and number, yet she could not bring herself to call him. Just as she started to tear up his note, the phone rang. "Hello."

"Hello Unique its David, how have you been?"

"I've been doing so much better, mentally and spiritually. Precious bought me a great easy to read Bible and I've been reading every day."

"Wow, GOD is so awesome!" he shouted with great joy. He invited Unique to his Church the following Sunday.

After attending for a few Sundays she became a member. She accepted Jesus Christ publicly as her personal Savior. She was saved that night she miscarried, however, she wanted to make a proclamation of her new relationship with God. She also wanted to join the Church fellowship.

"I'm so happy for you Unique! I praise God that you are saved! I knew I wasn't praying in vain for you girl!" They hugged. After church, they went out to eat and laughed and talked all about high school. David knew that GOD had brought Unique into his life to bless him as time went on and their friendship grew.

About four months had gone by and David prayed that GOD would tell him if she was to be his wife. Unique enjoyed her friendship with David. And she felt complete because of her relationship with GOD. She no longer felt a void because she didn't have a husband. GOD became her husband, her best friend, her father, her provider, her everything. The desire for a husband was there, yet it did not consume her.

One day, Precious and Unique were in her office talking. "So I wonder how long you and Dave are going to act like yall don't see what GOD is doing."

"Precious please." Unique turned her chair so precious didn't see her grin from ear to ear.

"No, Please Unique!"

"Ok, I love him, but what do you want me to do? The Bible does say *a man who finds a wife finds a good thing*, right?"

"Yes it does! Amen to that! I'm glad you are admitting your feelings though. Cause for a minute there I thought you were sleeping!"

"I have thought about it at times, but I don't think he is attracted to me in that way at all. He treats me like I'm his sister." Unique dropped her head.

"No sweetheart, it's just that he's a real man of GOD and he respects GOD's word and you. He is treating you like a sister because you are his sister. You're not use to that." Precious explained.

Unique got a call she had to take and Precious left. A few minutes went by and David walked in. "Hello everyone."

"Hello" everyone chattered.

"Unique and I are having lunch today; do you want to come Precious?"

"No thank you, but I would like to ask you a question.

Has GOD sent you a wife?" David laughed as his smile refused to stray from his face.

"Well I guess HE has, that's why I bought this."

He pulled out a five-karat diamond platinum ring in a lavender satin box and showed it to Precious. In shock, she almost hit the floor.

"Oh my goodness! Oh... Oh! How long have you had this?"

"Well for two weeks now. I told Unique I had a surprise for her this Sunday. I actually have two. I was studying to be a Minister and Sunday is my first sermon. Unique thought I was taking up more medical classes. So, before my sermon I'm going to propose to her in front of the whole congregation!" David smiled at his excellent idea.

"Oh well! You know we will be there! That is so awesome! That is so..." Unique walked out of her office.

"What is so awesome? Hey Davie!" She gives him a warm hug while waiting for Precious to answer.

"You guys are having lunch together today! That is so beautiful!" Precious hurried her way back to work to avoid any more questions.

Unique grabber her jacket, "You are silly; this is not the first time crazy!"

Precious started planning Unique's surprise bridal shower right away. All the while, she did not suspect a thing.

At lunch, David and Unique engaged in regular conversation. Then, as they ate, Unique's mind began to wonder off.

As I sit here in your presence, my heart is filled with many things. The moment you're in my view, something starts to ring. I'm afraid to confess my feelings, as if I were a child. Hiding my real emotions, keeping them in a private file. Earlier at my office today, my feelings were longing to speak. Yet, your presence took my breath away and my heart fell to my feet. You've never told me you wanted me or that you'd always be there. You've never promised me anything or even made your feelings clear. You've never told me your plans or what we may come to be. If I open up my heart, will that allow you to see?

The working week had ended and the girls went out to find Unique a nice dress to wear for church Sunday. Unique had no idea that David was going to teach or propose to her. She thought her great surprise was something like her favorite gospel singer was coming to the church or they were going to give her an award for being an outstanding youth ministry worker. Precious was not able to contain her smile as she praised GOD all that day. Unique found everything she needed at Polka Dots Clothing store and they called it a day.

Sunday morning came, all was going well. Unique sang and praised GOD for having brought her so far. Life had seemed hopeless and death seemed like her only escape at times. Now here she was, living in the arms of her Father and knowing that no matter what, He would always be there. No greater love had she ever known. Just as she was reflecting, The doorbell rang.

"What's up Precious, what are you doing here?"

"We are coming to your church today girl. We want to see this great surprise too!" Precious danced on the porch.

"Well that's what's up! I'll meet you there in about

twenty minutes."

"Ok!" Precious got back into her car with her family and pulled off.

When Unique arrived to her new church home, she was blessed to see a couple of her friends from work. "Finally, you guys came! I am so happy to see yall! You are going to be blessed today!"

Unique gave them a hug and took a seat in the third row where Precious and her family sat. David was nowhere in sight.

After the announcements, singing, and offering, David entered the Sanctuary and stood behind the pulpit. "Good afternoon everyone. I want to first praise and thank my GOD for being who He is. And thank you LORD for blessing me with the woman of my dreams and my hearts desires. Unique James, and unique she is." Unique could hardly keep her composure as tears of joy streamed down her face. That was one of those days she was grateful she never wore too much makeup.

"Wow, what a surprise this is" she thought. "David is going to preach today." Then as her heart pounded he said,

"Unique I love you so much with all of my heart and I couldn't imagine spending my life without you, so would you please be a blessing to my soul and be my beautiful wife?"

As David made his way down from the pulpit and headed towards Unique, she could hardly see his face. Tears flooded her eyes as her heart raced faster than ever before.

"Yes! Yes!" She screamed with excitement.

He presented the ring to her and she nearly hit the floor. Everyone stood and clapped and the choir began to sing. Everything seemed like a dream and Unique was so filled with joy. She broke out into a crazy praise, giving GOD all that was due to HIM. She screamed, she stomped, and she threw up her hands. She didn't care who thought what. Then, as David moved back and gave her room, she moved to the center and dropped to the floor. Some people whispered, "wow she must have really wanted to be married," but it was much more than that. She was supposed to die so many times and she knew death was what she deserved. Nevertheless, GOD had kept her, blessed, and protected her even when she didn't acknowledge His name. Now here she was alive and free. Moreover, to top things off, a man that she could only dream of was asking her to become his wife. She praised and praised and as she took her seat she continued to praise God as her new fiancée preached.

She worshiped GOD with all her might. Freedom was not only a dream, but it was her hidden mission in life. Now she had both freedom and her dream come true.

David and Unique were together almost every day as they planned their wedding. Unique planned to wear all

lavender and David all white with lavender shoes and tie.
Precious would be her matron of honor and she would have
two of her friends from work as her bridesmaids. They
would wear all white with lavender accessories. Precious's
daughter and son were going to be the flower girl and ring
bearer. They were to be married by their Pastor in a
beautiful park that had a little stream that flowed quietly
with rose petals in it.

After her bridal shower, Precious and Unique sat and
talked for hours. "I still don't understand why God has been
so good to me."

"Girl that is just the way He is. He loves us so much
and wants our lives to reflect His goodness. See, when
others peep that you have gone through all that you did and
now you are having a joy filled life, they want to know how
that can be. That's when you tell them and God receives the
glory. Then, they want to get to know Him. That's our time
to give them the Gospel. He allowed you to go through what
you went through and now you have to go and tell others
about His saving power. It was all worked out before you
were even born!" Unique got down on her knees to pray.

"He is so awesome," she shouted.

The big day had finally arrived. The sun was shining and the heat had taken a vacation. There was a soft breeze in the air as if it were a perfect fall day. No rain in sight and the sky was as blue as fresh water. Unique made her way down the walk way and everyone was in awe. She praised dance towards her new husband as Ribbon in the Sky by Stevie Wonder played softly. Although Unique's earthly father did not walk with her, her Heavenly Father was there all the way and she felt HIS presence. And she looked stunning. The second David set his eyes on her, tears ran down his face as he watched GOD's new creation. Who was that battered, confused, torn up woman that rushed into his life the day of her accident. Who was she? She was a broken fuzzy little caterpillar and now his butterfly, so beautiful and colorful. They both had prepared to recite their own vows. David looked lovingly into Unique's eyes, "I'm so glad you finally realized you were not created to remain a caterpillar and that you've started your new beginning. What GOD has joined together let no man separate. We are one forever, and ever. My love, my Blessing, my Unique Butterfly."

Fighting back her prevailing tears, she said softly,

"On this 13th day of July, I make these vows to you. I will always love you this deeply and remain forever true. When you came into my life, I didn't have a clue; GOD was in the midst of blessing me and making my heart brand new. I vow to always keep you first, summit, and understand. I vow to satisfy your needs and never let go of your hand. And I vow to always know my roll and respect you as my man. No matter what life may bring, or what GOD allows us to go through, I will always be your Butterfly, because you are my dream come true!"

When the Pastor said, "you may now kiss the bride", tears fell fast from both of their faces. They held each other for a while before they even kissed.

"I present to you for the first time Mr. and Mrs. David Sharp!"

They arrived a little late to the hotel where they had their reception. As they entered, everyone clapped, smiled and cried. Unique took the stage and caught David off guard.

"I would like to recite this poem to my husband, my lord, my blessing from my GOD. Dave, I love you so much!

No, I've never been loved like this before, I just know it's all that I prayed for. As the days drift by, you seem to love me more. You are the one that I shall cherish, the one that I'll adore. I never thought you could know me so well and treat me so right. But my faith allowed me to see what was

*not in my sight. And with GOD, our love will remain
consistent and tight. It's truly hard to be angry with you,
almost impossible to be mad. Because I see you as my little
savior, who has rescued me at last!"*

A year went by and the Sharp's were living life
abundantly. David lived in a condominium and Unique
wanted a new start so they both decided to move into a
brand new home. She became pregnant and they were so
happy. She found out she was having a boy and they
decorated the baby room to fit the new little man. Precious
had a surprise baby Shower for her and when the baby was
born, they named him David Jr.

Some time had passed and all was going well. Then,
one morning after David had left for work, Unique got a
knock at the door. She looked out of the peephole and
almost fainted. Why was he here? How did he find her?
What did he want? Apart of her was afraid, and then she
reminded herself of GOD's word. She knew that GOD did
not give her the spirit of fear! She opened the door. "Hello
Emmanuel, how did you find me?"

"Hi, can I come in?"

"Well, no... what are you here for?" She shut the door a
little.

"I came to see my baby. I want to be a part of his or her life. Is it a boy or girl?"

"Emmanuel we don't have a child, I lost our baby the same day you left."

"That's not true Unique, I saw you yesterday with our baby going down this street! Why can't I see my baby?" He started to raise his voice and get hostile. As Unique attempted to close the door, he put his foot in it.

"Look I just want to see the baby, why you want to keep them from me?"

"Listen Emmanuel, there is no baby of ours! I lost that child. This is my husband's child. He is only 8 months old! The timing is not even right. Please go." Emmanuel spoke with persistence,

"let me see him! Just let me see him!" He pushed on

the door and attempted to shove his way in. As they, struggled David drove up and jumped out of his car. He had forgotten his wallet and came back to pick it up. Unique screamed, "David its Emmanuel! He is trying..."

David grabbed Emmanuel by the back of his collar and threw him to the ground. "Unique call the cops!" He instructed her. Emmanuel in a state of shock tried to get up to run, but David threw him back down and held him down with his foot.

"What do you want with my wife and where do you get off coming to our house like this?"

"Man, I thought she had my baby and I was just coming to see him."

"Listen to this bro; nothing belongs to you here, got that? Don't ever in your life set foot on this block or near my wife again. Do we have that understanding?" Emmanuel shook as the boot in his chest slowed down his breathing.

"it's cool man, it's cool."

The police came and they filed a report and later a restraining order against him. This time he was gone for good. David held Unique close to his heart as she shook from still being in shock.

"No one will ever hurt you unless they kill me first baby, never." He kissed her forehead and it was as if peace was transferred from his lips into her soul. She was instantly at ease. No fear, just peace, comfort and safety. A feeling she never knew and a feeling that could only come from a relationship with GOD through Jesus Christ.

As a butterfly with wings can soar so high, as they flutter, sparkle, and they fly and fly, so was Unique. Free; yes, finally free. Oh, what a butterfly!

More about the Author

Authors Personal Testimony

I was born and named, but I wasn't supposed to make it. I was loved and claimed, but still, I wasn't supposed to make it. I was born In West Philadelphia to a seventeen year old girl who had epilepsy, and a father who had a drug, and alcohol addiction. My mother only lived eight months after I was born. I never knew her, nor could I remember seeing her face. Yet, I found myself crying for her many nights. This void in my life was supposed to destroy me, and I wasn't supposed to make it.

It was March 5, 1975 when my mother died in her sleep. You can say that my father died that day also, because he was the one who found her. So hurt and depressed, drugs and alcohol replaced me, and in that brief moment I was also fatherless. Unable to process the pain, he continued his addiction for my entire childhood. I grew up without an example of a real man, and as I searched for love, I always found pain.

When I turned 13, I started to seek love elsewhere. My grandmother no longer accepted me for who I was. She said things to me at times that caused scars no one on earth could heal. I was called a slut when I was still a virgin. I searched for anyone and anything to fill what she emptied.

Yet, I always found myself in pools of pain. I then began to try and drink my sorrows away.

Unable to handle me, she sent me to live with my father when I turned 14. I had maintained an F average that school year; my grandmother was at a lost. My father had been clean for a while. It seemed the best thing for me at the time. But, living with my father was very depressing. Later I was allowed to return to Philly. The truth, no matter the place, I was going to be unhappy. I just wasn't supposed to make it. I can still hear the strong, yet, powerless voices, "Why bother going to school, you'll still be dumb? You aren't worth nothing, and you'll never be nothing!" It's funny how you start to believe others and their opinions become your facts about yourself. If for a second you start to believe you are special, and important, you quickly tell yourself you're lying. I mean, everyone can't be wrong, can they? Then, your goals seem unobtainable, and your dreams seem unreachable. At times I believed in myself and my piers did also, it was when I stopped receiving acceptance from my grandmother that I shut down. When I knew she couldn't stand who I was becoming, something within me gave up and died. She would get so frustrated with me that she would lash out with harsh and hurtful words. "Slut, whore, tramp, dumb, fool." These words were supposed to remind me of who I was. I wanted to believe different, so I searched deeper and harder for someone, anyone to make me feel better about myself. Being loved and accepted was all that mattered to me. I grew to nearly hate my grandmother because she didn't display her love in a way that I could see. I searched for a love to replace hers. The pain from that only led me to attempt suicide.

Then I meet HIM, a guy who was not what, or who he said he was. All I wanted was love, all he had were lies. I believed that it was possible for someone to love, and accept me for who I was. I believed it was him. His lies made me feel wanted, special, important, needed, and somehow complete. Although our entire 3 1/2 year relationship was built on lies, it made me feel loved. He was the first guy that stayed around after sexual intercourse. And although he did something every week to cause me to want to leave him, he would promise me he'd die without me. He would fall to his knees begging, crying, and promising change. The words were powerful but the tears caused me to stay.

Six months into the relationship, things got crazy. Abuse became a normal way of communicating. I can't remember the first hit, there were so many fights. Make no mistake, I always fought back. He pushed, I kicked, he slapped, I scratched, he grabbed, and I punched. It was just terrible. I didn't realize that I was reliving the life that my mother and father had. Here was the cycle continuing. Even after all of the disrespect, fighting and cheating, I stayed. His verbal abuse caused me to believe that no one else would love, or accept me, no one but him. He also used verbal abuse to tear my self-esteem down. And with all the different STDs he had given me, I wondered, "Why would someone else want me?" We'd break up almost every two months or so and end up right back together. Hit after hit, fight after fight, girl after girl. I cried, and cried but lacked the strength and courage to leave. I use to pray that I would just die and never wake again. I wanted to escape but didn't know how. I had what it took to leave, but I choose to stay and believed his lies.

I moved into my own apartment with him at 18 and that didn't work out. I had to leave because I was lying awake at night planning how I would murder him in his sleep. I left, yet I didn't separate myself from him totally. And at the age of 19, I became pregnant. At that time we were not going together, but we still slept together. I had decided not to keep my baby because I didn't want anything to keep us connected. I made three different appointments to have an abortion, but due to financial issues, it never took place. By the time the money became available, I was already convinced by his tears to keep our baby. I thought it was rather strange that he wanted me to keep our child. Because when I was 5 months pregnant, he put his hands on me.

Being the fool that I was, I took him back and nothing changed. Throughout my entire pregnancy, he had unprotected sex with numbers of females. I was not in the dark about his cheating, I cried nearly every day. Only God kept my son alive and healthy, because if it was left up to my stress, he might not have made it. I regretted keeping my baby at that time because more and more I realized that I would be doing everything all alone.

After having my son, I started to feel needed, loved, and accepted. My son brought me strength and joy. The love that I had for my son was not shared by his father, so that made it easier to leave him. One day he became so unattractive that I couldn't even bear to see his face. So, after one more night out of him cheating on me, it was finally over forever. (Or so I thought.) I wound up pregnant again by him. But, I got an abortion five and a half months into the pregnancy. I left him for good shortly after that. That relationship was another trick that was supposed to destroy my life, my confidence, my dreams and my being. I wasn't supposed to make.

The struggle, pain, and obstacles that lied in front of me were endless. When I received enough physical, verbal, and mental abuse, I moved on to a few more abusive relationships. I didn't stay around as long as before because I knew I deserved better. While living in Rock Bottom, I tried things to lift me high, like, weed, alcohol, dust, Xanax, volumes, and prescription cough syrup. I thought being so high could keep me from feeling my pain.

When my grandmother died in July of 1996, it was time to answer the Lords constant call. It was at her funeral that I chose to give my life to Him. I still had a far and long road to travel. Somehow, I remained in bondage, and the devil kept getting victory instead of GOD. Then when I hit the bottom of rock bottom I was freed.

I was in a homeless shelter and I received some very serious counseling. I realized that the real problem wasn't men or sex. The problem was, I had made ACCEPTANCE my God, and my Lord wouldn't settle for 2nd place.

I was actually kicked out of the homeless shelter, but God used that experience to get me ready for the next phase in life, and I haven't looked back since. I now have a wonderful husband/best friend, and an awesome son! I am walking in Gods light, shinning everywhere we go! And despite the odds, I MADE IT!

The Art of Writing

You have something special you want to say, yet you can't find the right words. Or maybe you just don't have the time. Well I have just the right thing to say! I Write for Anniversaries, Weddings, Funerals, Mother's Day, Birthdays, Web Sites, and more!
www.theartofwriting.webs.com

Christian Rap Ministry

Mrs. Chosen is my name I use for my Christian Rap Ministry and I have built a website to sample a few of my songs that I've recorded at my home.

www.mrschosen.webs.com

The True Love Story

This is a site I built that tells the story of how my husband and I became one!

www.thetruelovestory.webs.com

Other Books

Find them at lulu.com/theartofwriting

Colors of a Butterfly is the autobiography of a girl, a woman, and a survivor! It has poems, letters, and journal entries, all from the heart and soul of a woman who decided giving up was not an option! Once you pick it up to read, you won't be able to find anywhere to put it back down!

"If we can't see past our present pain to focus on the bigger picture of Gods Glory, then our minds are wrapped up in the wrong thing!" – Lisa Gore

I Will Believe

I Will Believe

By Lisa Gore

"I Will Believe" is the first of many children's books to come that are created to help build healthy self-worth in young children. Each book has its own Believer Buddie. This story is from Amazing Amber

Made in the USA
Middletown, DE
31 July 2023